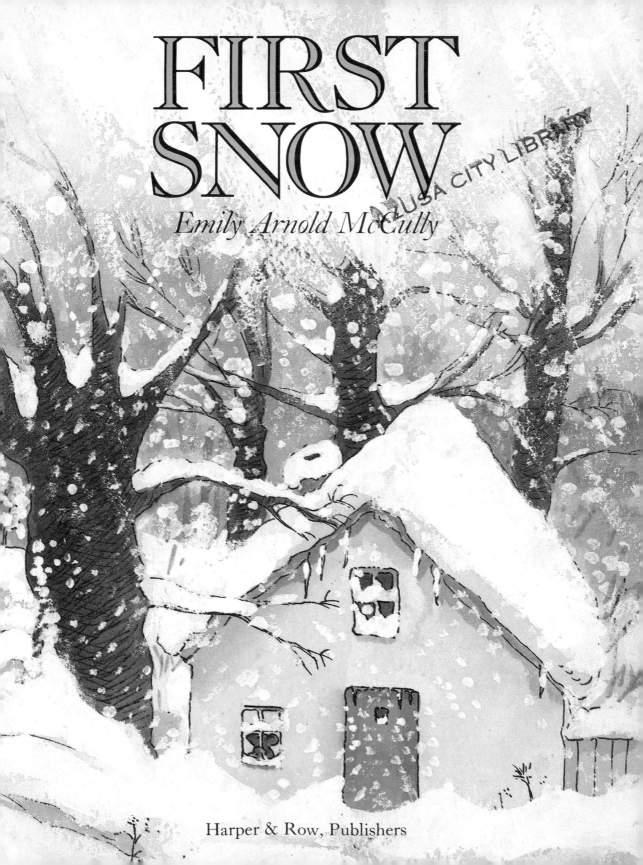

FIRST SNOW

Emily Arnold McCully

Harper & Row, Publishers

Copyright © 1985 by Emily Arnold McCully
Printed in the U.S.A. All rights reserved.
First Edition
Library of Congress Cataloging in Publication Data
McCully, Emily Arnold.
First snow.
Summary: A timid little mouse discovers the
thrill of sledding in the first snow of the winter.
1. Children's stories, American. [1. Mice—
Fiction. 2. Snow—Fiction. 3. Stories without
words] I. Title.
PZ7.M478415Fi 1985   [E]   84-43244
ISBN 0-06-024128-4   ISBN 0-06-024129-2 (lib. bdg.)